When I Met the Wolf Girls

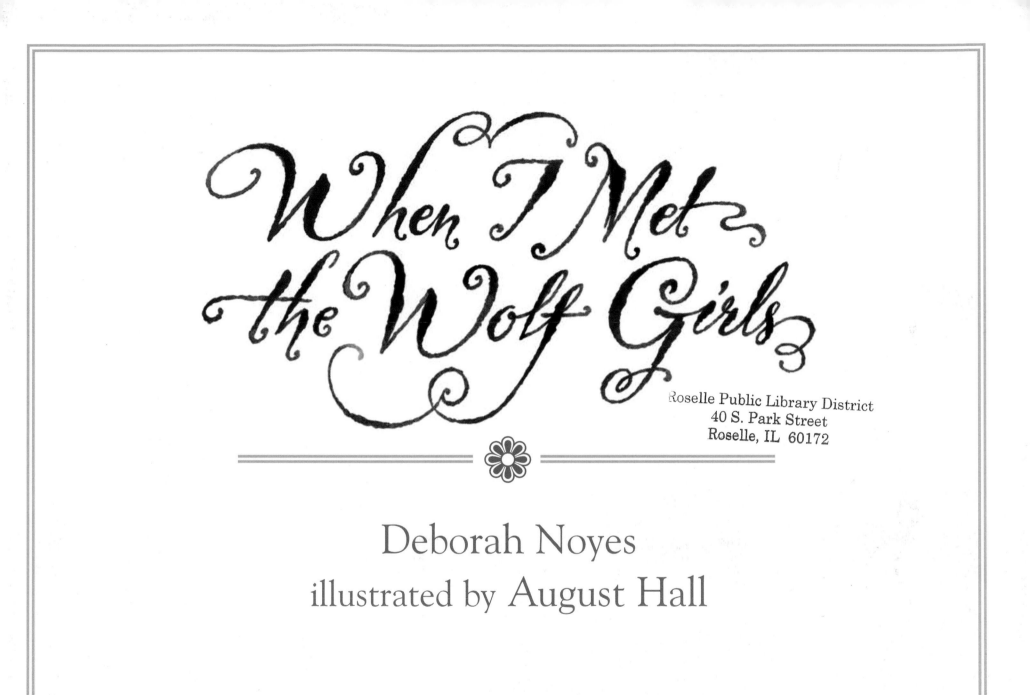

When I Met the Wolf Girls

Deborah Noyes

illustrated by August Hall

HOUGHTON MIFFLIN COMPANY · BOSTON · 2007

www.houghtonmifflinbooks.com

The text of this book is set in 16-point Goudy Old Style.
The illustrations were painted in acrylics.
Book design by Carol Goldenberg

Library of Congress Cataloging-in-Publication Data

Noyes, Deborah.
When I met the wolf girls / written by Deborah Noyes ; illustrated by August Hall.
p. cm.
Summary: Seven-year-old Bulu describes events surrounding the arrival of two wolf girls at her orphanage,
including attempts to teach them to eat properly and to speak.
ISBN 0-618-60567-3 (hardcover)
[1. Feral children—Fiction. 2. India—Fiction.] I. Hall, August, ill. II. Title.
PZ7.N96157Whe 2007
[E]-dc22
2005022805

ISBN-13: 978-0-618-60567-5

Manufactured in China
WKT 10 9 8 7 6 5 4 3 2 1

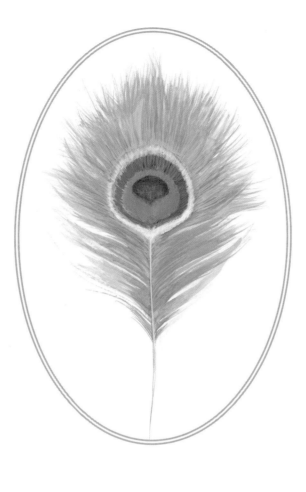

For Kate O'Sullivan—D.N.

❁

For Mom, Mike Bustamante, Judy Cook,
David Kang, and Garrett Hicks—A.H.

EVERY DAY AT THE ORPHANAGE,
after the day's spices were ground
and the mangoes peeled
and our godly lessons learned,
I — Bulu — marched
all but the napping babies
into the noon sun.

Out we spilled into the courtyard,
a parade of knobby brown knees
and clean-scrubbed hands,
clapping sticks together in song.

Down we went to the fence
at the edge of the jungle.
On the other side
lived big-clawed bears,
coiled pythons, and tigers with teeth,
but here by the dangerous fence
the Reverend and Missus Singh
and God could not hear us.

Because I was oldest,
I spoke the spell,
the same spell every day,
the one to keep the wild away.
Shadows black, stay back! I called,
leaning over the boards
into the blinking green.

Before the wolf girls came,
our world ended at the fence.

But one day a man
from beyond the village came,
calling the reverend "Sir."
He waved his clumsy hat
and croaked, *Man-ghost. Jungle.*
His words thrilled us.

So the reverend went.
Missus let us move our blankets close
that night in a candlelit ring
and sang us toward sleep,
sang over the wolf-song
sounding deep in the forest.

"Mother," sighed baby Mato,
and we all tugged at her sari
and threw off our sheets.
Missus only laughed:
"I have love enough for *all* of you."
She kissed and stroked
each stubbled head,
then blew out the candles.

We dreamed, in the jungle's embrace,
of mothers and man-ghosts,
tigers with teeth,
pythons and wolves,
deep in the forest.

Weeks went
and the expedition returned
with squirming bundles on a cart,
creatures wound in sheets,
one little and one not.
Tangle-headed and covered in sores,
they snarled when poked at.
"Wolf girls," said the reverend.
"Found with pups in a den
hidden in a termite mound."

Missus scrubbed them hard
and clipped away clumps of hair.
All day the wolf girls slept,
curled together,
or sat with their backs to us,
though we pleaded.
They ate licking the plate like dogs
and tore at their clothing.
Pacing all night, they plagued our dreams.
They never spoke or smiled.

The reverend scribbled in his diary.
"Sir," I said when he paused once,
"everyone wonders
when they will go."

"Hush, Bulu. I am writing."

Writing about the wolf girls.
Amala and Kamala.
Always the wolf girls.

"Don't they wish to be home?"

He smiled, saying,
"Our chatterbox, Bulu.
Always ready with words or a song.
Home is here — for all of us.
Kamala is your own age, almost eight.
See how she walks,
loping on all fours like a beast?
Together we will tame her,
rinse the jungle out
and fill her with God's mercy."

For weeks and months I tried.
I tickled her foot.
Kamala snarled.

I brought her a flower.
She showed her teeth.

I hummed her a tune.
Kamala dozed.

I sliced her a mango.
    She wrinkled her nose and
blew a feather from her lip.

In time, I understood.
I had forgotten
to speak the spell that day . . .
the day the wolf girls came.

So I ran out to the fence, shouting,
Shadows black, stay back!
Twice.

But it was the month of Asadh
so the black sky burst
and the monsoon came
roaring, ready to rinse
us from the jungle. "It's your fault,"
I told Kamala.
"We're stuck inside now."
But she would not look at me.

How could I know
that she was ill?
Amala too.
That Amala would not live.
When the doctor went, he watched
the elder wolf girl sniffing round
Amala's bowl and pillow.
He spoke politely of the new road,
of men with trucks and chains
beyond the village,
ripping down trees for miles.

Day after day, Kamala lay still
and would not touch her plate
or sat, unmoving, by Amala's.
Did Kamala dream of their wolf mother,
of her strong heart
beating through the warm fur?
You'll forget, I whispered softly
while she slept.
We all do.

Another monsoon season.
Another year.
Like the rest of us,
Kamala follows Missus to and fro.
She would wag her tail if she had one.
She has a few words now —
or parts of words —
but Kamala would sooner grunt.
She will never learn, I think.
Never smile.

One day during a break in the rains,
a peddler comes, his packs sagging.
He praises the new roads
and claims he has a treat for us.
"For the orphans,"
he says, "for a small fee."
It is called sky fire.

"Let the whole village come!"
chimes the reverend. "Tonight."

BOOM. HISS. CRACK.

There are gold sky spiders
and blue stars bursting.
Every face is raised.

I turn to the fence
and imagine them out there
among dark trees —
wolf and mongoose,
tiger and bear,
python and peacock —
staring through the jungle canopy,
the strange light
reflected in their eyes.

Kamala is not in the
courtyard with the others.
I find her indoors, in the dark,
whimpering.

Perhaps she would
speak her own lonely spell
to keep back the roads,
the men with chains and saws,
the boom and blaze of sky fire.

But she is a wolf girl
and has no words.

I have words enough for both of us.

Photograph used by courtesy of Centennial Museum, the University of Texas at El Paso

Author's Note

THOUGH BULU IS AN IMAGINED CHARACTER, Amala and Kamala, the wolf girls in this story, really did exist.

Recovered in September 1920 by the Christian missionary J.A.L. Singh, who ran an orphanage in Midnapore (a town in northwest India), the girls were first glimpsed in the jungle by villagers, who appealed to Singh to exorcise the "man-ghosts." The missionary formed an expedition and soon saw why witnesses had described these fleeting, small figures as phantoms. The children's bodies were plastered in sores and scars and their hair was hideously matted, obscuring all but their eyes, which Singh called "bright and piercing."

The feral girls had somehow survived with a female wolf and her cubs in a den concealed in a massive termite mound. When Singh's party split open the mound to get at the pair, the wolf fiercely defended her pups and charges, only to be killed in the struggle (Singh later praised the nobility of this "fond and ideal mother" in his diary).

The reverend brought Amala and Kamala to live at the orphanage, where he and Mrs. Singh gently tried to introduce the girls to life with the other children. At first, they scarcely seemed to hear human speech, though their senses were sharp and they could sniff out raw meat at some distance. If Kamala found a dead bird outdoors, she'd snatch it up in her jaws and flee into the bushes, emerging with a mouthful of feathers.

When Amala got sick and died about a year after their arrival, Kamala mourned inconsolably, nosing around the little girl's haunts and belongings for weeks and months afterward. In time, she responded to Mrs. Singh's affectionate efforts to "tame" her — learning to wear dresses, stand up straight with help, and use some thirty basic words — but Kamala went on eating and drinking from a dish on the ground and even took to visiting the orphanage dogs, who let her share their meals without protest. By the time she died of illness at about age seventeen, Kamala was still more at ease with animals than people.

Stories of wolves and other animals caring for human children have been around since ancient times. In legend, Romulus and Remus, the twin founders of Rome, were nursed as infants by a she-wolf, and accounts of "savage" children were common among British imperialists in the nineteenth century, probably inspiring Rudyard Kipling to craft his classic tales about the wild boy Mowgli, as in *The Jungle Book*.

Sources

Landau, Elaine, *Wild Children: Growing up Without Human Contact*. New York: Franklin Watts, 1998.

Newton, Michael, *Savage Girls and Wild Boys: A History of Feral Children*. London: Faber & Faber, 2002.

www.feralchildren.com

About the Author and Illustrator

Deb Noyes is the author of several books for young readers, including *One Kingdom: Our Lives with Animals*. She lives in Somerville, Massachusetts, with her family.

August Hall was born in Albuquerque, New Mexico. He has illustrated for Industrial Light and Magic, Pixar Animation, and Dreamworks. This is his first picture book.